The Best Cat Suit of All

Sylvia Cassedy

PICTURES BY

Rosekrans Hoffman

Dial easy-to-read

DIAL BOOKS FOR YOUNG READERS · New York

For the two Coldstream Guardsmen,
the Mexican duck,
and the can of bug spray.
S.C.

Published by Dial Books for Young Readers
A Division of Penguin Books USA Inc.
375 Hudson Street
New York, New York 10014

Text copyright © 1991 by Sylvia Cassedy
Pictures copyright © 1991 by Rosekrans Hoffman
All rights reserved
Printed in Hong Kong by South China Printing Company (1988) Limited
The Dial Easy-to-Read logo is a registered trademark of
Dial Books for Young Readers, a division of Penguin Books USA Inc.,
® TM 1,162,718.

Library of Congress Cataloging in Publication Data
Cassedy, Sylvia. The best cat suit of all.
Summary: Being in a new place for Halloween is bad enough,
but when Matthew has a cold and can't go out in his cat suit,
none of the visitors can cheer him up until the last one,
who is wearing the best cat suit of all.
[1. Halloween—Fiction. 2. Moving, Household—Fiction.
3. Cats—Fiction. 4. Sick—Fiction.] I. Title.
PZ7.C268515Bj 1991 [E] 87-24659
ISBN 0-8037-0516-6
ISBN 0-8037-0517-4 (lib. bdg.)

First Edition
1 3 5 7 9 10 8 6 4 2

The full-color artwork was prepared using pencil,
colored pencils, and colored inks.
It was then scanner-separated and reproduced
as red, blue, yellow, and black halftones.

Reading Level 2.2

Back where I used to live,

Halloween was wonderful.

For one thing, it was always

a nice warm day

on Halloween,

back where I used to live.

3

You could go outside
with just your cat suit on.
Here, you have to wear
a snowsuit underneath.
You have to wear
a big fat hat
under your cat ears.
You don't look
like a cat at all.
You look like a balloon
with a tail.

5

Back where I used to live,

everybody gave out good stuff

to eat on Halloween.

Here, all you get

are apples and raisins.

So your teeth won't rot.

Also, back where I used to live,

I had a best friend

to go out with on Halloween.

Betsy was a witch

and I was her black cat.

We made our costumes ourselves

and they were wonderful.

Betsy's was a long black T-shirt

and a black paper hat.

The hat had a moon on it.
Mine was black pajamas
with black socks
for my front paws.
I wore black paper ears
that stood up stiff and tall,
as if they were
waiting for a mouse.
The tail was a long black sock
with a towel inside.
Everything was black, in fact,
except for my hind paws.
They were white
with red and blue stripes.

When we got to somebody's door,

I would get down

on my hands and knees

and say, "Meow."

Betsy would cackle like a witch.

She would feed me my candy.

Here, I have to go out alone—

if I get to go out at all.

Back where I used to live,

I didn't get sick on Halloween.

I didn't have to stay home

and blow my nose,

while everybody else

went trick-or-treating.

"It won't be so bad, Matthew,"
my father told me.

"You can be an *indoor* cat
this year.

"You can curl up

on the chair

under a nice warm blanket,"

he said.

"You can look at all

the costumes that come to the door.

You can purr,

just like a real cat."

"Real cats purr

when they're happy," I said.

"I'm not happy.

I'm sick.

My nose keeps running."

But I put on my cat suit anyway.

I curled up on the chair

under a blanket.

I rubbed my nose with a paw.

Pretty soon the doorbell rang.

"Well, well, well," my father said.

"Look, Matthew.

It's a ballerina

and a pink camel.

What nice toe shoes,"

he said to the ballerina.

"Nobody wore green toe shoes

back where we used to live."

They weren't toe shoes.

They were her galoshes.

And the camel wasn't a camel.

It was a rabbit.

The hump was its snowsuit hood.

"They looked dumb," I said
when they were gone.
"Nobody looked like that
back where we used to live."
I blew my nose.
The doorbell rang again.

"Well, well, well," my father said.
"Look, Matthew.
It's a lot of little Santa Clauses."
"No, it isn't," one of them said.
"It's Snow White
and the Seven Dwarfs."

19

"So it is," my father said.
"And that's a lucky thing,
because I just happen to have
some dwarf food."
He gave them each
a box of raisins.

"Weren't they nice, Matthew?"
he asked.

"Nobody was Snow White

and the Seven Dwarfs

back where we used to live."

"They were dumb," I said.

"Snow White was just

somebody's father.

All he had on

was his father suit.

And there weren't seven dwarfs.

There were four.

Besides, their beards

were coming off."

I blew my nose some more.

The bell rang again.

"Well, well, well," my father said.

"A witch and a black cat."

And this time he was right.

"Look, Matthew.

The cat is just like you.

Except this one has red paws."

"It is NOT just like me,"

I said.

It wasn't.

The pajamas weren't even black.

The ears were crooked.

The tail was just a bathrobe belt.

But the cat got down

on its hands and knees,

just like me.

It said, "Meow,"

just like me.

"Hey," I called out.

"You can't do that!

That's *my* trick!"

My father scratched the cat

under its chin.

"How about a nice

bowl of milk?" he asked.

"I'm allergic to milk,"

the cat said.

It took a box of raisins

and walked out

on its hind legs.

"That was a dumb cat suit,"
I said.

"The pajamas were dumb.

The paws were dumb.

The tail was dumb.

You could see the pin."

After that a lot of

witches and black cats came.

The cats all got down

on their hands and knees.

They all said, "Meow."

My father asked them

if they wanted

a bowl of milk.

I pulled the blanket

over my head.

29

For a while

everything was quiet.

But then the bell rang again.

"Well, well, well,"

I heard my father say.

"Here is someone

in a mother costume.

Let's see.

She has on a mother coat

and a mother hat

and a mother pocketbook.

Oh, and mother shoes too.

My, my, my.

How ever do you walk

in those things?"

I looked up.

It was my mother,

coming home from work.

"Trick or treat,"

she said to me,

so I gave her a kiss.

But then I began to cry.

"This is a terrible Halloween,"

I said.

"I'm sick.

The costumes are dumb.

They have snowsuits under them.

Betsy isn't here."

I blew my nose.

"I want to be back

where we used to live."

"Well, now," my mother said.

"Things aren't that bad.

We can have our own Halloween.

We can have a fire in the fireplace.

We can roast apples.

We didn't have a fireplace

back where we used to live.

We couldn't roast apples.

You can sit by the fire,"

she said, "and be our cat.

You can have

a nice bowl of milk."

"I don't want a nice
bowl of milk," I said.
I followed her
into the kitchen.
"I want something
to rot my teeth."
The doorbell rang again.

"Well, well, well,"

I heard my father say.

"A witch and a black cat!"

Again.

"Trick or treat,"

one of them said.

"Let me see," my father said.

"Here is a box of raisins

for you.

And how about a bowl

of milk for your cat?"

"We're not together,"

the witch answered.

I heard her go away.

The cat said, "Meow."

"Well," my father said.

"That's a nice tail you have.

What did you

stuff it with?

And the pajamas are nice too.

How come your mother

didn't make you wear

a snowsuit underneath?"

The cat said, "Meow," again.

"Hey, Matthew," my father called out.

"Come and see this cat suit."

"I don't want to," I answered.

"They all look alike."

"This one's different,"

my father said.

"You can't see the pin."

"I don't care," I said,

but I went in anyway.

The black cat

was lying on the rug.

"Hey," I said.

"Look at that!

Look at THAT!

That is the best cat suit

I have seen all night!"

And it was!

No pins.

No snowsuit.

Nice ears.

Better than mine even.

I got down

on my hands and knees

so we could look at each other,

cat to cat.

"Say," I said,

"how about a bowl of milk?"

The black cat said, "Meow."

He followed me

into the kitchen.

"Happy Halloween," I said.

The cat drank the milk all up.

Then we curled up

in front of the fire,

like two indoor cats.

"You know what?"

I said in his ear.

"Next Halloween,

I'm going to change my costume.

Next Halloween,

I'm wearing all-black sneakers.

So we can be twins."

My father roasted an apple

in the fire.

"This is a nice Halloween,"

he said.

And it was.

Better even than back

where we used to live.